Jack and Jill
and other rhymes

Illustrated by Pamela Storey

Contents

GONDOLA

Jack and Jill went up the hill
To fetch a pail of water;
Jack fell down and broke his crown,
And Jill came tumbling after.

Up Jack got, and home did trot,
As fast as he could caper,
He went to bed, to mend his head
With vinegar and brown paper.

Hey diddle diddle,
The cat and the fiddle,
The cow jumped over the moon;
The little dog laughed
To see such sport,
And the dish ran away
  with the spoon.

Little Jack Horner
Sat in the corner,
Eating a Christmas pie;
He put in his thumb,
And pulled out a plum,
And said, "What a good boy am I!"

Hickory, dickory, dock,
The mouse ran up the clock.
The clock struck one,
The mouse ran down,
Hickory, dickory, dock.

Sing a song of sixpence,
A pocket full of rye;
Four and twenty blackbirds,
Baked in a pie.

When the pie was opened,
The birds began to sing;
Was not that a dainty dish,
To set before the king?

The king was in his counting house,
Counting out his money;
The queen was in the parlour,
Eating bread and honey.

The maid was in the garden,
Hanging out the clothes,
There came a little blackbird,
And snapped off her nose.

Yankee Doodle came to town,
Riding on a pony;
He stuck a feather in his cap
And called it macaroni.

Wee Willie Winkie
  runs through the town,
Upstairs and downstairs
  in his night-gown,
Rapping at the window,
  crying through the lock,
Are the children all in bed,
  for now it's eight o'clock?

One, two,
Buckle my shoe;
Three, four,
Knock at the door;
Five, six,
Pick up sticks;
Seven, eight,
Lay them straight;
Nine, ten,
A big fat hen;

Eleven, twelve,
Dig and delve;
Thirteen, fourteen,
Maids a-courting;
Fifteen, sixteen,
Maids in the kitchen;
Seventeen, eighteen,
Maids in waiting;
Nineteen, twenty,
My plate's empty.

Jingle, bells! Jingle, bells!
Jingle all the way;
Oh, what fun it is to ride
In a one-horse open sleigh.

Old Mother Hubbard
Went to the cupboard,
To fetch her poor dog a bone;
But when she came there
The cupboard was bare
And so the poor dog had none.

Bye, baby bunting,
Daddy's gone a-hunting,
Gone to get a rabbit skin
To wrap the baby bunting in.